HAWK & CROW

Collision in the Sky

An Easy to Read Children's

Picture Book or Early Chapter Book

About an Unexpected Friendship

Between Two Birds

Written & Illustrated by Marcie Gibbons

Dedicated to
"Golden Friendships"

Book design by Serelda Elliot, serelda.elliot@gmail.com

Photography by Kathy Plunket Versluys, www.idopics.com

Printed by CreateSpace

ISBN: 978-1470026547

Additional copies available from
amazon.com and other retailers.

To contact Marcie Gibbons,
visit her on Facebook or email
hcstories409@gmail.com

Table of Contents

I. Collision

Bo Crow lived by the river in a willow tree.
"I wonder what's happening west of here," he said
to himself. He took off, looking for some fun.

Hamilton Hawk lived up in the mountains in a
hickory tree. "I wonder what's happening to the
east," he said to himself. He headed out, looking
for adventure.

Bo was looking down. He did not see Hamilton. Hamilton was looking down. He did not see Bo. They crashed into each other and fell from the sky.

Luckily, they landed in a bush. Bo landed feet up. Hamilton landed feet down. "Why didn't you look where you were *going*?" yelled Hamilton.

"Why didn't *you* look where you were going?" shouted Bo.

"Get your foot out of my face!" shrieked Hamilton.

"Get your foot *off* my face!" cried Bo.

They tumbled out of the bush and landed next
to a stream. Sparkles of light danced on the
rippling water.

"It's hot today," said Hamilton.

"Yeah," said Bo.

"I'm going to cool my feet," said Hamilton.

"Good idea," said Bo.

They both leaned back on a rock.

"Nice spot here," said Hamilton, stretching his toes underwater.

"Yes, very nice," replied Bo, as his feet splashed the surface.

They spent the afternoon talking while minnows scurried past.

The air cooled as shadows stretched. Jumping up on the rock, Hamilton said, "You know, hawks and crows don't usually get along."

"True," said Bo, hopping up to face him, "but… it's been fun."

"Yes, an interesting time," said Hamilton. "Maybe I'll see you again."

"Yeah, maybe," said Bo.

They looked each other up and down. Then Bo flew back to the east, and Hamilton flew back to the west.

II. The Contests

The next day, Hamilton was flying high in the sky. Far below, he noticed a crow flying above the road.

"Oh, it's Bo, I guess I'll say 'Hi.'"

Hamilton went into a dive. Bo saw a big shadow coming at him. He somersaulted into the ditch.

"What do you think you're *doing*?" asked Bo, as he shook some dirt from his feathers.

"Just doing my morning exercises," said Hamilton.

"Well, I bet you can't do this," said Bo. He did two spins in the air.

"Not bad," said Hamilton, "but try this." He did two front rolls.

"That's nothing," said Bo. "Watch me." He did a
backward roll with a twist.

"I bet I can fly higher than you," said Hamilton.

"No way!" said Bo.

They shot up into the sky. Bo gasped for breath as he struggled to keep up.

"Beat you to the road!" said Bo, then he went into a dive.

"Hey, you had a head start!" said Hamilton, plunging after him.

Bo had to swerve as a car sped by.

Over the hill, a whistle blew. "Can you beat a train?" shouted Bo.

"Every time," said Hamilton, wondering how fast trains could go.

They both flapped with all their might and managed to stay ahead of the engine.

Exhausted, they stopped at a roadside drain for a drink.

"Funnnn," said Hamilton.

"Yeahhhh," said Bo.

"Did you ever fly at night?" asked Bo

"No," said Hamilton.

"Want to? I hear ghosts fly at night."

"Uh, sure," said Hamilton.

"You're not scared are you?"

"Let's meet at ten o'clock tonight at the rock by the stream," said Hamilton.

"I'll be there," said Bo.

III. Night Flight

The full moon shone brightly
on the warm summer night.
Hamilton got to the rock first. He
did not see Bo. He listened for a
while to the buzzing of the
katydids in the trees.

"I bet Bo isn't coming. Guess I'll
go home."

Just then the grass moved and
a big shadow slid over the rock.
Hamilton fell backwards.

"What's the matter, Hamilton?"
asked Bo, as he stepped out into
the moonlight.

"Oh hi… just lost my footing,"
said Hamilton. He scrambled back
up on the rock.

When a bullfrog hit a low note, they both jumped. "It sounds different at night," said Hamilton.

"Yeah, and everything looks different too," said Bo. "This place gives me the creeps."

"Me too," said Hamilton. "Let's fly!"

They flew low. They flew in zigzags. They soared high. They made big circles. They saw raccoons, possums, snakes, and…

... a glowing-eyed creature coming right at them!

"It's the GHOST!" yelled Bo.

"I'll see you later!" called Hamilton. They sped off in opposite directions.

"WHOOOOOoooo … was that?" asked Owl as
he soared into the night.

IV. Bo Visits Hamilton

Bo stood on the rock by the stream and gazed at the sky. No Hamilton; only drifting clouds.

"I wonder where Hamilton lives?" he thought aloud. Then he took off, heading toward the mountains.

By the time he stopped on a rocky ledge, the land had become quite steep. The view was great, except for some dirt that was falling in his face. He coughed, then looked up.

High above him in a hickory tree, Hamilton was sweeping his porch.

"Hey Bo," shouted Hamilton, "come on up!"

Bo noticed flowers growing in window boxes. He sat down on a stool shaded by a green umbrella. "Nice place you got here," said Bo.

"Thanks! You're just in time for brunch," said Hamilton. "I'll be right back."

Hamilton brought out a tray with drinks and tiny meat cakes. Bo stuffed three cakes in his mouth. "*Thethe are grae!*" he said, spewing crumbs.

"Glad you like them," said Hamilton. "Hey, how about a game of chess?"

"Well, I know checkers," said Bo, "but you can teach me chess."

They competed for an hour. "Check-mate," said Hamilton. "That's it, Bo. I win, but you played a good game."

"Yeah, I did, didn't I," said Bo.

"C'mon inside," said Hamilton.

"Alright," said Bo, wondering what would happen next.

"Let's listen to music," said Hamilton. He put
on some opera. He sat down in a chair and closed
his eyes. His wings moved in time to the music.

Bo had never heard this kind of music before. When it got loud, he stood on his head and kicked his feet. When it got quiet, he rolled like a rolling pin across the carpet. He accidentally rolled into Hamilton. Hamilton's eyes popped open.

"Do you like opera?" asked Hamilton.

"Yes, it's very moving," said Bo. "But now I feel like moving outside. How high is this mountain?"

"I'll show you," said Hamilton. "Follow me."

They flew up to the peak. From there they could see the whole valley with the stream where they met, the town, and the river.

"See that clump of willow trees by the river?" asked Bo. "That's where I live. Come see me some day," he added. Then off he went.

"I will," called Hamilton. He watched until Bo became a mere speck in the distance.

V. Hamilton Visits Bo

Hamilton was gliding high. A strong wind pushed him east. He spied some willow trees at the river's edge. "This must be where Bo lives," he said to himself.

He landed on a willow branch. Something metal was going *clink... clink.* Down below he saw Bo and two of Bo's relatives. They were pitching horseshoes.

As he leaned over to get a better look, the branch snapped. Hamilton fell right into the middle of the game. A horseshoe whizzed past his head.

"Hamilton," laughed Bo, "so nice of you to drop in! Grab some shoes and join us."

"It looks like fun," said Hamilton, leaping to his feet. "Okay, I'll give it a try."

The first one he threw was too long. The second one was too short. The third one was a ringer.

"Awesome!" said Bo. His cousins, Ed and Catfish, nodded.

"Who's hungry?" asked Bo, pointing to the steaming black pot. "Help yourselves to some crayfish stew."

Ed, Catfish, and Bo grabbed bowls and filled them to the rim. Hamilton scooped a small amount into his bowl. It looked strange, but it smelled really good. He finished his quickly.

They all went back for more and more until the pot was empty.

"That was *stew*…pendous!" said Hamilton.
Everyone laughed.

Catfish picked up an empty jug and started to blow on it. Ed beat on the stew pot with some sticks. Hamilton tapped two spoons together on his leg. Bo plucked the strings on his banjo and sang some lively tunes. They played and played until the crickets began to sing along, too.

"It's getting late," said Hamilton. "I better get going. Thanks for a great time!"

"See you soon, I hope," said Bo.

"Yes, soon," said Hamilton.

"And hey, watch out for that ghost on your way," called Bo, as Hamilton sailed off into the sunset.

A Friend Can Be Anyone
by Marcie Gibbons

A friend can be anyone,
    So look and see.
Someone in the room's a
    Possibility.

A friend can be anyone.
    Where will it happen?
In the hall, on the field,
    Or sky like Bo and Hamilton.

A friend can be anyone
    So how do you know?
A smile or a look
    Can let it show.

CHORUS

A friend can be anyone, tall or short.
A friend can be anyone, boy or girl.
A friend can be anyone, young or old,
Black, white, tan, brown; friends are gold!

A friend can be anyone
    You see every day.
Don't be afraid to say...
    "Come and play!"

A friend can be anyone
    That likes what you do.
No limit to how many,
    Who spend time with you.

A friend can be anyone,
    So take the *dare*.
Then just give it time,
    You'll have a lot to share!

REPEAT CHORUS

CPSIA information can be obtained at www.ICGtesting.com
Printed in the USA
BVIW12n1205110417
480957BV00004B/14